Dear mouse friends,
Welcome to the world of

Geronimo Stilton

The Editorial Staff of
The Rodent's Gazette

1. Linda Thinslice
2. Sweetie Cheesetriangle
3. Ratella Redfur
4. Soya Mousehao
5. Cheesita de la Pampa
6. Mouseanna Mousetti
7. Yale Youngmouse
8. Toni Tinypaw
9. Tina Spicytail
10. Maximilian Mousemower
11. Valerie Vole
12. Trap Stilton
13. Branwen Musclemouse
14. Zeppola Zap
15. Merenguita Gingermouse
16. Ratsy O'Shea
17. Rodentrick Roundrat
18. Teddy von Muffler
19. Thea Stilton
20. Erronea Misprint
21. Pinky Pick
22. Ya-ya O'Cheddar
23. Mousella MacMouser
24. Kreamy O'Cheddar
25. Blasco Tabasco
26. Toffie Sugarsweet
27. Tylerat Truemouse
28. Larry Keys
29. Michael Mouse
30. Geronimo Stilton
31. Benjamin Stilton
32. Briette Finerat
33. Raclette Finerat

Geronimo Stilton
A learned and brainy
mouse; editor of
The Rodent's Gazette

Thea Stilton
Geronimo's sister and
special correspondent at
The Rodent's Gazette

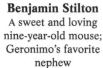

Trap Stilton
An awful joker;
Geronimo's cousin and
owner of the store
Cheap Junk for Less

Benjamin Stilton
A sweet and loving
nine-year-old mouse;
Geronimo's favorite
nephew

Geronimo Stilton

PAWS OFF, CHEDDARFACE!

Scholastic Inc.

New York   Toronto   London   Auckland   Sydney
Mexico City   New Delhi   Hong Kong   Buenos Aires

TC

4-15-06 12.00

ISBN 0-439-55968-5

Text by Geronimo Stilton
Original cover by Matt Wolf; revised by Larry Keys
Illustrations by Mark Nithael and Kat Steven
Graphics by Merenguita Gingermouse and Marina Bonanni
Special thanks to Kathryn Cristaldi
Cover design by Ursula Albano
Interior layout by Kay Petronio

12 11 10 9 8 7 6   5 6 7 8 9/0

Printed in the U.S.A.   23
First printing, April 2004

A WHACKING IN THE MORNING . . .

It all started one morning. I was on my way to the office when I was stopped by an elderly female rodent. No, she didn't stop me to ask the time. Or to get my autograph. Oh, did I tell you? I am a best-selling author and I run a newspaper called *The Rodent's Gazette.* Maybe you have heard of me. My name is Stilton, *Geronimo Stilton.*

Anyway, as I was saying, this mouse was not a fan. She was the exact opposite. One minute, she was staring me in the snout, and the next, she'd

Geronimo Stilton

pulled out her umbrella. Then she whacked me over the head!

I was in shock. "What was that for?" I squeaked.

The mouse just stamped her paw. "Young mouse, you have some nerve! Have you forgotten about the bus stop?" she shrieked.

I shook my head. I had no idea what this mouse was talking about.

"You stepped on my paw on Monday morning!" she insisted. "And you didn't even bother to apologize. How rude!"

Without another word, she stalked off in a huff.

I didn't know what to make of it. I had never seen that mouse before in my life!

"You have some nerve!"

Un-be-liev-a-ble!

TROUBLE AT THE NIBBLER

I headed toward the **SUBWAY**. At the station, I ran into a friend of mine. His name is Benny Bluewhiskers, but most rodents call him the Big Cheese. That's because he knows everything there is to know about CHEESES — COLOR, size, shape, texture. He even invented Mouse Island's famous cheese measurer. And his nose is the most famous sniffer on all of Mouse Island. He can smell a cheese danish baking a mile away. What a schnoz! What a gift!

As soon as he saw me, Benny frowned. "Some friend you are, Geronimo!" he cried. "How could you do that to me last night?"

cheese measurer

BENNY BLUEWHISKERS

I looked at him, confused. "Last night?" I repeated. What had I done last night? Oh, yes, I had spent the evening watching television. I am not usually a real TV mouse, but sometimes I like *Tales of Rodents Past*. Last night, I saw this episode about cave mice. It was fascinating.

I started to tell Benny about the show, but he didn't seem interested.

"Nice try, Geronimo," he snorted. "But you weren't watching TV last night. You were making fun of me down at *The Nibbler*."

Now I was really confused. *The Nibbler* is a popular diner in town. Sometimes we mice go there for coffee and to shoot the cheese. But I hadn't been there in months.

"I know I'm not the thinnest rodent in town, but you didn't have to call me a furry whale with a tail!" Benny shrieked. "You really hurt my feelings, Geronimo. After all these years, I thought we were friends."

I looked at him in shock. Cheese niblets! "But I wasn't at *The Nibbler* last night," I tried to explain.

That seemed to make Benny even madder. "So now you're calling me a liar!" he squeaked. "Well, that's it! No more free cheese for you! And you can forget my holiday cheddar log this year, too!"

I didn't know what to say. My head was spinning faster than the cyclone at the Mouseyland Amusement Park.

Un-be-liev-a-ble!

TELL US ALL, YOU RASCAL!

I stumbled into my office, still in a daze. What was going on? Was I losing my mind? Why was everyone picking on me?

Right then, the phone rang.

"Hello? Stilton speaking, *Geronimo Stilton*!" I answered.

It was Simon Squealer. He was the most famous radio host in New Mouse City. His show was all gossip. I hated that stuff. I mean, who cares about these silly scandals and rumors? I would much rather read a good

SIMON SQUEALER

book than listen to that trash. So I wondered why Simon was calling me.

"Today we are squeaking to Geronimo Stilton, best-selling author and publisher of the popular newspaper *The Rodent's Gazette,*" the host began babbling. "Yes, you're on the air, Stilton!" he finished.

I gulped. Me? On the radio? "D-d-did you s-s-say on the air?" I stammered.

Simon just chuckled.

"What a paw-puller. You're the one who set up this interview!" he laughed. "Remember you called me on Friday? You said you had some juicy gossip you wanted to tell the public? Some big secret about yourself? Well, go ahead. My listeners are waiting. What is it?"

I chewed my whiskers. This was crazy. I never called Simon Squealer. I didn't have any juicy secrets to reveal to the public.

"I really don't, um, have anything to um, say . . ." I mumbled.

But Squealer wouldn't let me go. "Don't be shy, you rascal," he insisted. "Come on, tell us everything.

Every shocking detail!"

I didn't know what to do. Should I make up some gossip? Should I come up with some terrible scandal? Nothing juicy ever happens to me. My sister, Thea, always tells me I'm as boring as a slice of plain American at a gourmet cheese shop! No, I couldn't make up a story. But I had to do something. Quickly, I grabbed a handkerchief from my pocket and I put it over the phone. Then I pretended there was static over the

line. "SORRY, I think we must have a bad connection," I lied. Then I hung up.

My sister may think I lead a boring life, but today was not one bit boring. It was getting wackier by the minute. First an old mouse clocks me over the head with her umbrella. Then an old friend chews me out. And now this. I didn't know what to make of it.

Un-be-liev-a-ble!

CHOCOLATE CHEESE BITES

The phone rang again. I was afraid to pick it up. But the ringing wouldn't stop. It was giving me a mouse-sized headache. At last, I gave in.

"Hello, Stilton speaking, *Geronimo Stilton*!" I squeaked.

A snooty voice came over the line. "Yes, this is Samuel Stuffymouse from **SWEET SELECTS**. Your chocolate cheese bites are ready. Do you want them gift-wrapped or will you be eating them today?"

Chocolate cheese bites? I hadn't ordered any chocolate. I mean, I love chocolate and cheese as much as the next mouse, but I was on a diet. I had started it last week. So far, I had only cheated once. My aunt Sweetfur had sent me a pineapple cheesecake. How could I resist? I love cheesecake!

Now I stared at the phone. "I'm SORRY," I told the mouse on the other end. "You must have the wrong rodent. I didn't order any chocolates."

Stuffymouse snorted. "I am a very busy mouse, Mr. Stilton," he huffed. "I don't have time for games. Of course you ordered them. You were in SWEET SELECTS just yesterday. Now, do you want this chocolate gift-wrapped or not?"

I didn't know what to say. Why wouldn't anyone listen to me today? "But I've never even heard of SWEET SELECTS," I tried to explain.

Samuel Stuffymouse

For some reason, this made Stuffymouse even more annoyed. He began squeaking at the top of his lungs. It seemed his store sold SPECIAL GOURMET CHOCOLATES. Each chocolate cheese bite was made by paw. Some were even shaped like things. There were tiny mice, tiny cats, and even tiny trains. "You ordered five pounds of our tiny tugboats!" he shrieked in my ear.

I felt faint. I don't even like boats! They make me queasy! Un-be-liev-a-ble! But Stuffymouse wasn't taking no for an answer. "My delivery rat is on his way," he snarled. "Please have your money ready."

Seconds later, I heard a loud honking outside. I peeked out the window. I should have guessed. It was the SWEET SELECTS truck. A mouse dressed in a tuxedo carrying a large box jumped out.

My bookkeeper, Ratsy O'Shea, led him into my office. She handed me my checkbook. What could I do? I had to pay for the chocolates. Old Stuffymouse would have my tail if I refused. Besides, how expensive could a box of CHOCOLATES be? Then I saw the bill. I began crying like a rat who's found his Christmouse stocking filled with coal instead of cheese.

"Are you OK, Mr. Stilton?" Ratsy asked.

I coughed. I had to pull myself together. I couldn't let Ratsy see me this way. After all, I am a professional mouse. I picked up the bill and wiped my eyes.

I had never seen so many zeroes in my life!

"I'm fine, Ratsy," I sobbed. "Just fine."

Un-be-liev-a-ble!

DOWN THE TOILET!

I decided I needed to get some air. I left the office. I bought a magazine at the newsstand. It was one of those mouse-hole improvement guides.

AND THAT'S WHEN I SAW IT.

It was an ad for a toilet called the Flusher Rat. But it wasn't the toilet that caught my eye. It was the rodent standing next to the toilet. **IT WAS ME!** That's right, yours truly, *Geronimo Stilton*, in the fur! In the picture, I was pointing to the toilet and grinning like I'd just won the Mouse Lotto.

My heart began beating wildly. What was going on? What was my picture doing in a magazine?

I looked closely at the ad. "My name is

"YOU'LL FEEL LIKE A KING ON A THRONE WITH FLUSHER RAT."
— Squeak! Words of Geronimo Stilton!
"What class!"
"Beware of imitations."
FLUSHER RAT
for the sophisticated mouse
in fine stores

Stilton, *Geronimo Stilton*!" it said. "I am a sophisticated rodent. I want the best for my mouse hole. That's why I have a Flusher Rat. There is no other toilet like it! In fact, I've had some of the best ideas for my books right here on the Flusher Rat!"

I cringed. Even my whiskers were blushing. How embarrassing! I sat down on the curb to think. Just then, a truck rolled by. I glanced up. Plastered to the side of the truck was a huge color poster. I squeaked. It was another picture of me and the Flusher Rat! There were posters of me and that rotten toilet stuck up all over the city!

FLUSHER RAT
for the sophisticated mouse

the posters read.

I couldn't believe it. I was famouse. Famouse for going to the bathroom! I was

so upset. I felt used. I felt cheap. My life was
going straight down the toilet!

Un-be-liev-a-ble!

A THICK-HEADED FURBRAIN

I headed home. I had to find out what was going on.

A crowd of rodents was waiting in front of my mouse hole. "**There he is!** That's him!" I heard them shout.

Oh, no. They must have seen the posters of me and the Flusher Rat. Maybe they wanted to ask me about toilet paper.

A reporter stuck a microphone under my snout. "Mr. Stilton, I am Colin Chattermouse from *Mouse TV*. Do you really believe that watching TV is better than reading a book?" he asked.

"Cheese niblets!" I squeaked. "That's ridiculous! Why would I, *Geronimo*

Stilton, say such a thing? I am the publisher of *The Rodent's Gazette,* the most popular paper in New Mouse City. I am a best-selling author. Only an **IGNORANT, ILLITERATE, INCOMPETENT, UNEDUCATED, THICK-HEADED FURBRAIN** would say something so foolish!"

But before I could go on, the reporter waved a newspaper under my snout. "Then how do you explain this?" he challenged. I gasped. The front page showed a picture of me holding a remote control in one paw. In the other paw, I held up a garbage can. It was filled with books! STILTON SAYS, "BOOKS ARE FOR BABIES, TELEVISION IS OUR FRIEND!" the headline read.

Just then, the phone rang. I picked it up. I shouldn't have. The rodent on the other end gave me some horrible news. I was being kicked out of the *Press Club*. "No respectable newspapermouse would throw away books!" he snorted.

"But I didn't do it!" I tried to protest. Still, it was too late. I was listening to a dial tone. The *Press Club* had hung up on me and my membership! **Un-be-liev-a-ble!**

STILTON, OLD PAL . . .

I was miserable. Then I noticed the light blinking on my answering machine. I raced over to it. Maybe I had some **happy messages**. Maybe my favorite nephew had called. Or perhaps my sweet Granny Onewhisker. Or maybe I'd won that free vacation to the Hamster Islands. I'd bought a raffle ticket just last week at the Shop and Nibble. Maybe I was about to get lucky.

Excited, I pressed the button on my machine. But I was wrong about the messages. They weren't happy at all. They were horrifying!

The first message was from some rodent named Stuart Swingtail. He said he was a

singer at the **SLEAZY FUR DANCE FACTORY!**
I frowned. I'd never been there. Only sewer rats hung out at the Sleazy Fur. So what was this Swingtail mouse calling *me* for?

Stuart Swingtail

"Hey, Stilton, old pal! You were really kicking up those paws Saturday night!" he squeaked. "By the way, you owe me fifty smackers. Don't forget, pal. See you next week at the factory!"

The second message was from Dr. Edward S. Smugrat III. He was a very rich and STUCK-UP mouse. He had the best golf clubs, the best golf shoes, and the best golf shirts. Still, he was an awful golfer. I guess it's true what they say, clothes do not make the mouse.

DR. EDWARD S. SMUGRAT III

"Stilton! What do you think you are twying to pull?" Smugrat shrieked. "I know you swiped my Wat King cwedit card! I just got the bill for your dinner with fifty-seven fwiends at the **golf club**. You will be heawing fwom my lawyer!"

After that came a message from a Mr. Van Der Raten. He owned an antiques shop called Treasured Crumbs. The antiques in his place were more expensive than my cousin Brainypaw's college tuition!

Still, Mr. Van Der Raten said that I had purchased a solid-gold cheese holder just yesterday. "I gave you the cheese holder on good faith," he said. "I know you are a respectable newspapermouse. But you will need to come in to settle your bill."

Mr. Van Der Raten

Swissita Tenderfur

Finally, there was a message from my sister's friend Swissita Tenderfur. "Geronimo, what was up with you yesterday?" she sniffed. "I know you saw me at the movies. I was sitting two seats away.

Why didn't you say hello? You were so rude!"

I slumped onto my couch. Could this day get any worse? I felt like a young mouse in Squeaking School who'd just been scolded by all of my teachers.

I didn't know what to make of it. **Un-be-liev-a-ble!**

I Thought You Hated Bikes

I decided to call my sister, Thea. She is a special correspondent for my newspaper, *The Rodent's Gazette*. Thea loves to pick on me. And she loves to give me advice.

THEA STILTON

"Hello, it's me," I said when she picked up the phone.

Immediately, my sister started giggling. "Gerry!" she chuckled. "You were looking pretty sharp yesterday on that motorcycle. I saw you on the corner of Blue Cheese Avenue and Fur Line Drive. That was some **WHEELIE** you pulled. When did you get the cycle? I thought you hated bikes."

I sighed. Even my own sister thought she

had seen me. But, of course, it wasn't me on that bike. I hate motorcycles more than the double-decker roller coaster at Scampertown Fair!

I told Thea the whole story. She listened carefully. Then she hung up on me. I couldn't believe it. My own sister didn't even want to talk to me! Five minutes later, the phone rang again. It was Thea. "I've made an appointment for you with a psychiatrist," she said. "I'll pick you up right away."

The psychiatrist's name was *Dr. Furry Feelgood*. He had thick glasses and a funny little beard. A sign on his wall read, DON'T WORRY, KEEP SQUEAKING!

I began to tell him my story. "What do you make of it, Doctor?" I finished anxiously.

He crossed his paws over his belly. "This looks like a **SPLIT PERSONALITY CASE...**

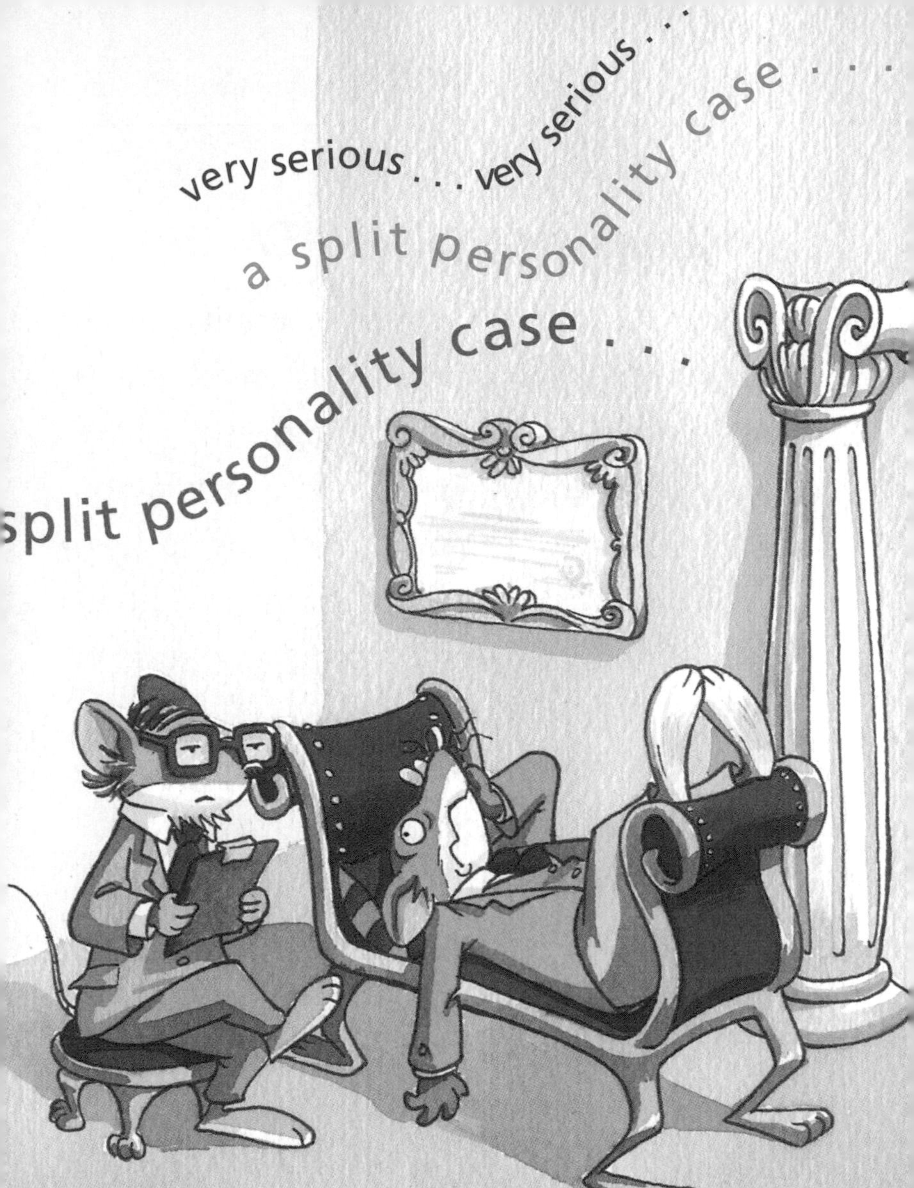

Dr. Furry Feelgood

...SPLIT PERSONALITY CASE

...very serious...very serious," he concluded. "You don't remember the things you have done...the things you have done...whom you have met...whom you have met...it is as if there were two Geronimo Stiltons...two Geronimo Stiltons ...this may take years of therapy...years of therapy."

I shook my head. Was he repeating himself? Or was I hearing double, too? **WHO KNOWS?**

I left the office feeling **discouraged**. Even Dr. Feelgood couldn't make me feel good.

You don't remember the things you have done... the things you have done... whom you have met... whom you have met...

MAY I HAVE YOUR AUTOGRAPH?

"Don't worry, big brother," my sister reassured me as we headed back to the office.

Just then, a strange mouse approached us. "Are you Geronimo Stilton? May I have your autograph?" he asked. "It's for my nephew. We're going to your **show** tonight. I love the dance numbers. Where do you get those moves? You're hilarious!"

My jaw hit the ground. Dance moves? **What was he talking about?**

At that moment, I noticed a poster stuck up on the side of a building. Was it? Could it be? Holey cheese! It was! Yes, it was a picture of me!

Holey cheese! Holey cheese! Holey cheese!

Geronimo Stilton Live Onstage! the poster read.

I didn't know what to make of it. I'm not an entertainer. I'm not even good at public squeaking!

At that moment, my sister tapped me on the shoulder. "I think I may have figured out how to solve your problem," she said.

"How?" I asked.

"Tonight we're going to the theater," she announced.

I scratched my head. I love the theater, but I wasn't really in the mood for it tonight. Besides, how would that solve my problem? "You have tickets to a show?" I asked. "Is it a musical? Is it a comedy?"

"No, you nincompoop! We're going to see your show!" Thea screeched. "Geronimo Stilton Live Onstage!"

Geronimo Stilton

LIVE ONSTAGE!

LIVE ONSTAGE!

at the
Pawprint Theater
7:30 p.m.

Don't miss Geronimo Stilton in this musical extravaganza!

Dancing, Squeaking, Cat Jokes, and more.

It's fun for the whole furry family!

LIVE ONSTAGE!

LIVE ONSTAGE!

LIVE ONSTAGE!

IDENTICAL, JUST LIKE TWIN MICE!

Applause, please!

We got to the theater early. It was packed. In an odd way, I was flattered. All of these rodents had come to see me, *Geronimo Stilton*.

A drumroll signaled the start of the show. A mouse appeared on the stage. "You all know New Mouse City's most famous publisher, *Geronimo Stilton* . . ." he began.

The crowd clapped.

"Mr. Stilton is not just a respected

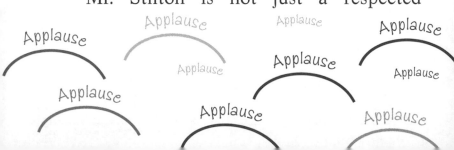

Applause Applause Applause Applause
Applause Applause Applause
Applause Applause Applause

newspapermouse, he is also a great performer!" the mouse continued.

Applause. More applause.

"So please put your paws together and welcome the unique, the amazing, the one and only *Geronimo Stilton*!" he exclaimed. The lights dimmed. A single spotlight lit the stage. Suddenly, a furry rodent jumped out of nowhere. He bowed to the crowd.

I gasped. It was me! I mean, it wasn't me, it was **HIM!**

I glanced at my sister and saw the same shocked look on her face.

"You are absolutely identical! Just like **twin mice!**" she whispered.

Meanwhile, the mouse onstage was busy greeting the crowd. He looked so smug. It gave me chills!

YOU ARE AS SWEET AS A BOWL OF CREAM . . .

The crowd was cheering like mad. I stared at the mouse onstage. What did they see in him, I wondered? I mean, I'm not an ugly rodent. But I'm no Mel Gibsqueak, the famouse movie mouse.

The other me threw his hat into the air. Then he began to tap-dance. He looked ridiculous.

Un-be-liev-a-ble!

The other me started singing onstage.

You are as sweet as a bowl of cream.

You are every rodent's dream.

Thinking of you I melt with glee.

You are just my cup of teeeea!

I snorted. What a silly little song! How

could I, I mean, he, embarrass himself like this? I waited for the crowd to start booing. But nothing happened. Instead, the crowd began squeaking. Squeaking with delight!

The lady mouse sitting next to me had her paw on her heart. "Oh, he is sooo romantic!" she shrieked hysterically. "What a mouse, that Stilton!"

I turned to my sister. I knew Thea wouldn't fall for this trash. She had too much taste. She had too much class. She had her eyes glued to the stage!

The other me ended his number with a bow. His female admirers threw him roses. He picked them up one at a time. Then he laid them on his

You are as sweet as a bowl of cream.

His female admirers threw him roses. The other me picked them up and laid them on his heart.

heart. The crowd shrieked with excitement.

I didn't know what to make of it. **Un-be-liev-a-ble!**

The heavy yellow curtains came down. He disappeared behind them with a grin.

A few minutes later, he came out again. This time, he was dressed in a funny little skirt made of bananas. He had a pineapple on his head for a hat. Then he began singing and shaking a pair of maracas.

Follow my tips,
Rotate your hips!
Wiggle your belly
Like some cheese jelly.
Come take a chance,
Do the tropical dance!

He then performed a couple

Do the tropical dance!

of dance routines. He did the pawstep, the fur fling, and the mouse trot. The crowd was applauding nonstop! I had never seen anything like it. I felt like I was at a Ricky Rodent concert. That mouse was more popular than frozen cheesecake in the summertime!

After that, my double launched into a wild *cha-cha-cha* cheese step. The whole time he sang this silly song.

One-two-three,
Cha-cha-cha!
Ched-da-ree,
Cha-cha-cha!
Melted brie,
Cha-cha-cha!
Munch-like-me,
Cha-cha-cha!
Un-be-liev-a-ble!

My lookalike changed his outfit once more. This time, he had a red rose between his teeth. He danced around the stage, blowing **KISSES** at the audience.

"*Olé! Olé! Olllllllléééééééé!*" he cried. Was he supposed to be a rat bullfighter? I could not get over his act. It was so bad I could have burst out laughing . . . or crying. After all, what if rodents thought that was me? He was awful. But the crowd loved him.

They cheered and clapped as if he were the greatest thing since Larry Labpaw invented spreadable cheddar!

Olé! Olé! Olé!

I didn't know what to make of it. **Un-be-liev-a-ble!**

Next, he came onstage wearing a tuxedo. He sang an aria from an opera. I

38

think it was in Italian.
But who knows? Maybe
he was just making up some
nonsense words. I wouldn't put
anything past this mouse.

Ah, l'amore!

Once again, he disappeared
behind the curtains. He came back
and began to rap.

Your-fur-is-so-soft,
Your-whiskers-so-fine.
If-I-grill-a-cheese-sandwich,
Will-you-be-mine?

This was entertainment? I was ready to
run squeaking from the theater. And yet, I
seemed to be the only unhappy one.
The crowd was applauding like mad.
They were even dancing on the chairs!
It was a never-ending performance.

Un-be-liev-a-ble!

Will-you-be-mine?

To gnaw . . . or not to gnaw?

The next time he came back onstage, he was dressed as a serious actor. He sniffed the air with a grim expression on his snout. Then he began to recite from a play by William Shakespearrat.

To gnaw . . .

Or not to gnaw?

That is the question!

Finally, he came out dressed as a **clown**. He had a red cherry taped to his nose. A huge piece of Swiss sat on his head.

Ha! Ha! Ha!

He told a few jokes. They were very old knock-knock jokes. I had heard them all before. I thought this time he definitely would be booed.

He was so awful. He was so pathetic.

I looked around at the crowd. He was getting a standing ovation!

I didn't know what to make of it. **Un-be-liev-a-ble!**

After the show, I was dying to meet the scoundrel snout-to-snout. So Thea and I waited near the actors' dressing rooms. After a while, my lookalike came out. He was whistling. In one paw, he clutched a huge wad of bills.

I was so angry I could hardly see straight. This miserable rodent was getting rich off my name! I leaped in front of him. "How dare you pass yourself off as me?!" I shrieked at the top of my lungs.

SYDNEY STARFUR

"*CHEWY CHEDDAR CHUNKS!*" he cried.
Then he raced away down the dark hallway.

I ran after him, but he was too fast for me.

He had dropped something, though. It
was a wallet. Thea plucked it from the floor.
"Let's see who this joker really is!" she said.

She opened the wallet and took out a
business card. It read, "**Sydney Starfur**,
professional actor. Singing, dancing, voices,
and more!"

Then she pulled out some crumpled-up
letters. They were from Sally Ratmousen.

I gasped. My fur stood on end. Sally
Ratmousen is **MY NUMBER ONE ENEMY!**
She runs *The Daily Rat*, a terrible newspaper.
It's filled with lots of made-up stories. Last

week, they had one about a pair of alien mice. It said the mice had landed in New Mouse City. Of course, none of it was true. Still, some rodents like to read *The Daily Rat*. In fact, it is my newspaper's biggest competition.

Now I shook my head. I should have known that rotten Sally Ratmousen was behind all of this! It looked like she had hired Sydney Starfur to pretend he was me. I chewed my whiskers. Sally was not only evil, she was also clever. She must be cooking up some terrible plan. But what?

un-be-liev-a-ble!

THE DAILY RAT

14 Cream Cheese Court

New Mouse City, Mouse Island 13131

To T.C.F.R.A.
(The Center for Rodent Actors)

Dear Sirs,

I need an actor who looks exactly like Geronimo Stilton. He is the publisher of *The Rodent's Gazette*.

Money is not important (sort of), if you can find a match.

Let me know.

Right now! At once! Immediately!

Sally Ratmousen

P. S. Don't tell Stilton.

THE DAILY RAT

14 Cream Cheese Court

New Mouse City, Mouse Island 13131

To Sydney Starfur

Dear Mr. Starfur,

I received your picture. You seem to be Geronimo Stilton's spitting image. You poor ninny. I will pay any amount (sort of) if you will play the part of that moron.

Let me know.

Right now! At once! Immediately!

Sally Ratmousen

WHAT A BIG, BIG MISTAKE!

That night, I had a terrible dream. I was onstage, singing, dressed in a skirt made of bananas.

The next morning, I was so tired I slept right through my alarm. I hurried down the stairs and raced into the diner. I have my breakfast there every morning. The owner, Flip Hotpaws, seemed surprised to see me. "Back for more coffee, Mr. Stilton?" he said.

I blinked. "What do you mean?" I asked, confused. But I was so late I didn't wait for an answer.

Next, I raced over to the newsstand. I picked up a paper.

Flip Hotpaws

Bobby Babblesnout stared at me from behind the counter. "Mr. Stilton, you already bought your paper *this morning*," he squeaked.

I shook my head. "That's impossible!" I protested. "I just got here. You must be confusing me with another mouse."

Bobby Babblesnout

Bobby frowned. "I never forget a customer," he insisted. "Besides, you've been coming here for the past twenty years. I'd recognize your snout anywhere!"

I didn't have time to argue, so I put down the paper and headed toward my office.

When I got there, the door was locked. I knocked. Thea stuck out her snout. When she saw me, her eyes opened wide. "How dare you show up here!" she shrieked.

"Well, you can just take your tail somewhere else! The **REAL** Geronimo Stilton is already inside!" She slammed the door in my snout.

I knocked again. "Thea, open the door, please, it's me!" I cried.

She opened the door again. "Go away, you **impostor!**"

Now I was really worried. Even my own sister didn't know me. "But it's me, Thea, your brother!" I insisted. "Don't you recognize me?"

She gave me a closer look. For a minute, she seemed about to change her mind.

I straightened my tie. I picked up my briefcase. I was ready for work. But then, through the half-open door, I saw something horrifying.

It was me, I mean, him, I mean, the fake Stilton sitting behind my desk!

"Of course I know which one of you is the real Geronimo . . ." my sister was muttering.

When they caught sight of me, my employees began whispering furiously. "That's Mr. Stilton's double," they said to one another.

My secretary, Mousella, shook her head. "Cheese niblets! He doesn't look like him at all!" she squeaked. "The real Stilton is this one!" she said, pointing to the mouse sitting at my desk.

The impostor

With that, my sister slammed the door in my snout . . . again. "Buzz off, Furface!" she shouted. "And don't you dare come back!"

A HOLELESS
MOUSE . . .

I went back home. When I tried to open the door, the key wouldn't fit. Someone had changed the lock!

I couldn't believe it. *How could this be happening to me?*

I was a good mouse. I never bothered anyone. I went to work. I paid my taxes. I volunteered down at the Holeless Shelter. Holey cheese! Now I was a holeless mouse, too! I guess it's true what they say. It could happen to anyone!

One by one, I called all of my closest friends. Unfortunately, Thea had already warned them about me. They all slammed the phone in my ear. They thought I was him, I mean, the fake Geronimo Stilton.

I called my cousin Trap. I got his obnoxious answering machine. "SQUEAK YOUR NAME AND NUMBER AND IF YOU'RE LUCKY I'LL GET BACK TO YOU," it said. How typical. My cousin really was one disturbed mouse.

Last of all, I tried to call my favorite nephew, Benjamin. He's only nine years old. He was in school. But the principal said I was not allowed to squeak with him. Rancid rat hairs! My sister must have warned him, too!

I decided there was only one thing left to do. I hid outside my hole. Then I waited for the fake Geronimo Stilton to show up.

Finally, I saw a yellow car approaching. That rotten mouse was driving MY car! He jumped out and checked my mailbox. Then he pulled my keys out of his pocket. What a rat! I jumped out just as he opened the door. "PAWS OFF, CHEDDARFACE!!!" I shrieked. "Paws off my home, my office, my family, my friends!" I was furious! I was enraged! I was staring at my own front door! "Poisonous cheese puffs!" I screamed. That sneaky fake had slipped by me again. He had already slammed the door in my snout!

I didn't know what to make of it.

Un-be-liev-a-ble!

Feeling cold and discouraged, I wandered the streets of New Mouse City. Oh, how I missed my cheese-filled fridge. Oh, how I missed my great-aunt Ratsy's cozy comforter. Oh, how I missed my life!

I wandered the streets of New Mouse City.

So long, Stilton!

After ten years, the sun came up. Well, OK, maybe it was only ten hours. Still, it felt like I'd been sulking in the dark forever.

The city was slowly waking up. Rodents rushed by on their way to work. Taxis raced down the streets. Everyone was going somewhere, doing something.

I sighed, feeling **VERY SAD**. I had NO home. I had NO work. I had **NO** family, NO friends. I was like a smelly sewer rat at a big party. No one wanted to dance with me. I was an outcast in my own town!

I stuck my paw in my pocket. I found some change. Cheesecake! At least I wasn't totally broke. I could buy myself a newspaper. I love reading the news.

But when I got to the newsstand, I nearly fainted. The front page of every newspaper was the same. The headlines read,

So long, Stilton! Hello, Sally!

I picked up the paper with shaking paws. Then I began to read. The article said that I had signed a secret agreement with Sally Ratmousen. Sally was now the owner of my paper, *The Rodent's Gazette*! I didn't know whether to laugh or cry. It was all so crazy.

It seemed Sally had bought my paper for next to nothing. Mice everywhere were shocked. Especially all of the mice at *The Rodent's Gazette.*

Sally was now the owner of my paper, *The Rodent's Gazette!*

Sally had fired them all. She had even fired my sister! How rude! How low! How evil! *"The Rodent's Gazette is* mine, **mine, mine!"** Sally had said when the deal was done.

By now, steam was pouring out of my ears. I was so angry I couldn't even squeak! So this is what Sally was up to all along. She had hired the fake Geronimo just to get her paws on my paper! Now everyone thought I had sold my priceless **RODENT'S GAZETTE**!

I chewed my whiskers, deep in thought. I had to come up with a plan. I had to get my paper back. I had to let Sally know the "S" in Stilton doesn't stand for simpleton!

Sally Ratmousen

 mine

 mine

mine mine

 mine

AUNT STITCHY'S
BIRTHDAY PRESENT

I ran to my office building. But when I got
there, I saw the most horrifying sight. My
beloved **RODENT'S GAZETTE** sign was stuffed
in a trash can! A humongous new sign was
hanging in its place. It read, **THE DAILY RAT**.

I called my sister right away.

"Thea, it's me!" I squeaked.

She snorted. "Which me? The real one or
the fake one?"

"Thea, it really *is* me," I
insisted. "I am your brother,
Geronimo Stilton!"

She snorted again. "Not
so fast, Furface," she said.
"First you'll have to take

my test. If it's really you, you'll know the right answers."

"OK, I'm ready," I declared. "Will I need a number two pencil?"

"No, you nincompoop!" Thea shrieked in my ear. "It's not that kind of test." Then she asked me if I remembered what my aunt Stitchy had given me on my fifth birthday.

I chuckled. Aunt Stitchy loved to knit. On my fifth birthday, Aunt Stitchy knit me the most **HIDEOUS YELLOW HAT**. "Remember? It had ears like a cat," I told Thea. "I looked ridiculous in that thing."

Thea as a child

Geronimo as a child

CHEESE-SCENTED BATH SALTS

Thea gave a sigh of relief. "It really *is* you!" she cried.

At last, I was getting somewhere. At last, someone believed I was me. I mean, the real me, *Geronimo Stilton*.

I told Thea how I had spent the night outside. I was tired and hungry. Plus, I really needed to take a bath. My fur was sticking up all over the place. How embarrassing!

Thea invited me over. I was at her door in a few minutes. My sister's house looks like a mouseum. All the walls are painted different colors: **cherry red, strawberry pink,** apple green, lemon yellow. It has a super-high ceiling and four indoor balconies.

*In the center of Thea's living room
stands this tall tropical plant.*

Yes, that's right, indoor balconies. Each balcony is made out of solid G L A S S. When you stand on them, you feel like you are floating. Thea's friends love them. But not me. I get too dizzy. I'm afraid of heights!

In the center of her living room stands this tall tropical plant. I don't mean tall like Dribble Fur, the famous basketball rat. I mean tall like New Mouse City's tallest skyscraper. Forget the watering can. Thea has to water that thing with a jumbo garden hose!

Besides plants, my sister loves artwork. Her walls are covered with *paintings*. Thea loves modern artwork. She has a picture of a mouse with two heads and one of a tiny cat stuck in a mousetrap. They're all sort of weird, if you ask me. I guess I'm more of a traditional mouse. I like my rodents with just one head. And I don't really like looking at mousetraps. I'd rather look at a picture of cheese.

Speaking of cheese, Thea had a cheesy surprise for me. She had filled the bathtub with some of her most expensive cheddar-scented bath salts.

I was in mouse heaven.

Cheesecake! I just love the smell of cheddar!

I put on the yellow sweatsuit that Thea had laid out for me. Then I went into the kitchen. Thea was making me breakfast. Pretty incredible for my sister. She can cook, but she'd rather not. Her drawers are filled with every take-out menu in the city. I was feeling pretty special. Thea can be really nice when she wants to. Too bad she never wants to.

I Am So Sorry, Geronimo . . .

Thea made a delicious meal — scrambled eggs, cheese, bacon, and toast. She even whipped up a mozzarella-flavored milk shake. A whisker-licking-good treat!

I ate like a prison mouse home for the holidays. I was like a machine on high speed. When I was done, I even licked my plate. Then I wiped my snout with a napkin.

"You have no idea what I've been through," I told my sister. "I slept on a park bench in the bitter **cold**. . . ."

OK, maybe I was laying it on a bit thick. But I did have a horrible night. An owl had kept me up past midnight. And my favorite

Thea made a delicious meal—
scrambled eggs, cheese, bacon, and toast.

green suit was now terribly wrinkled. And I had just had it dry-cleaned!

Thea listened to my story. When I finished, there were tears in her eyes.

"I am really sorry, Geronimo," she sniffed. "I should never have slammed the door in your snout. But that mouse was so believable. He was just **LIKE YOU**. He walked **LIKE YOU**. He talked **LIKE YOU**. He even nibbled his whiskers when he got nervous **LIKE YOU**!"

HE WAS JUST LIKE YOU.

HE WALKED LIKE YOU.

HE TALKED LIKE YOU.

DEAREST UNCLE GERONIMO!

I put my paw around my sister. *"It's OK,"* I told her. "I'm just glad you believe me now."

Right then, my young nephew Benjamin burst through the door. He ran toward me. Then he gave me a big hug.

"Uncle Geronimo! Auntie Thea told me that a wicked mouse tried to trick us. He tried to take your place," he cried. "But no one could ever take your place, Uncle Geronimo. You're the best uncle ever!"

I grinned. "Thanks, my dear Benjamin. And you are the best nephew ever."

Minutes later, the doorbell rang. This time it was my cousin Trap. Do you know him? Trap loves to tell awful jokes. And he loves to play pranks on me. Still, he is a relative. And he does have a soft side. Sometimes . . .

Of course, today Trap was as obnoxious as always. He strolled into Thea's house as if he owned it. He was stuffing his face. Oh, yes, one other thing you should know about my cousin. He loves to eat. Anything. Anytime.

"Thanks, my dear Benjamin. And you are the best nephew ever."

Anywhere. This time it was chocolate Cheesy Chews. He popped one after another into his mouth. Then he wiped his sticky paws on my sister's fancy designer pillows.

"Heard about your double trouble," Trap squeaked. "But don't worry, Cousinkins. That lookalike mouse couldn't fool me. I'd always recognize you. How could I forget that *STENCH!* Hee, hee, hee."

I rolled my eyes. Did I mention my cousin can be extremely irritating? Normally, I would have been furious. But I was so happy to be with my family again that I decided to let it go.

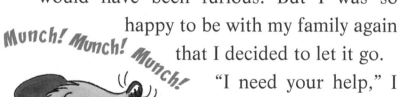

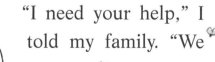

Munch! Munch! Munch!

"I need your help," I told my family. "We

have to get *The Rodent's Gazette* back. We have to come up with some kind of scheme, some kind of strategy."

Trap nodded in agreement. "Yes, that's right," he muttered. "We need some kind of cream, some kind of sight to see."

Now it was Thea's turn to roll her eyes. "It's *scheme* and *strategy,* Trap," she corrected him.

"Whatever," he said, waving his paw in the air. "Hey, I have an IDEA. We wait for this fake Geronimo to show up. Then we punch his lights out!"

Thea rolled her eyes. "No violence, Trap!" she scolded. "It's uncivilized!"

Trap scratched his head. "It's one shoe size?" he muttered. "Who's talking about shoes? I know you love shopping for shoes, but we're trying to help Geronimo now.

Really, Thea. Get with the program!"

With that, my sister began screaming at Trap. They chased each other around the house. Those two are like mold and cheese. They just don't get along.

I watched the two of them fighting. Meanwhile, I was deep in thought. I was so angry with Sally Ratmousen and her fake Geronimo. I still could not believe my lookalike had fooled everyone. Even my family! "What a scoundrel!" I muttered out loud. "That mouse practically cloned me!"

All of a sudden, Benjamin jumped up.

"I'VE GOT IT, UNCLE!" he squeaked.

"LET'S USE SALLY RATMOUSEN'S TRICK.
ALL WE HAVE TO DO IS FIND A MOUSE
THAT LOOKS JUST LIKE HER!"

DO I HAVE A PIMPLE ON MY SNOUT?

It was a great idea. We would get back at Sally using her own trick. But where would we find a mouse who looked like Sally?

Just then, I noticed that Thea was staring strangely at Trap.

She looked him up and down. "Same height, same weight," she MUMBLED. "We can bleach his fur. We can do the nails. Add some fake eyelashes and makeup . . ."

I stared at my sister. Was she right? Could Trap really play the part of Sally Ratmousen? Well, he could definitely do the obnoxious

part. Still, it all seemed so crazy. So wild. So nutty. So unbelievably brilliant! Yes, I decided, it was such a ridiculous idea it just might work!

I winked at my sister. Benjamin grinned. We all slapped paws. "Let's do it!" we cried.

Of course, Trap was the last to catch on. "*What's going on?*" he squeaked. "Why are you all staring at me? Is my fur messy? Are my whiskers twisted? Do I have a pimple on my snout?"

Thea giggled. "*No time to explain*, Cousinkins," she said. Then she pushed him out the door.

TIMOTHY T. TIDYTAIL

We dragged Trap to Thea's beauty salon, **Fur 4 Life**. A sign in the window read,

*WE DO MORE THAN JUST FIX FUR.
WE FIX THE WHOLE MOUSE!*

We were welcomed by Timothy T. Tidytail. Tidytail clapped his paws together when he saw Thea.

"Oh, Miss Stilton, how nice to see you!" he gushed. "You look absolutely *fabumouse*, darling!"

Thea smoothed her fur, flattered. She'd been coming to **Fur 4 Life** for years. They did her fur. They did her

Timothy T. Tidytail

"We have an emergency here!"

nails. Once, they even did her laundry. Thea was one of Tidytail's best customers.

Today, she grabbed his paw. "I need your help, Timmy," she squeaked.

Tidytail smiled. "Of course, Miss Stilton," he said. "What do you need done today? A manicure? A massage? An American cheese omelet to go?"

"It's not for me, Timmy," Thea murmured. "It's for my cousin here."

In a low whisper, Thea explained the whole story to Tidytail. He nodded, staring at Trap.

Five minutes later, my cousin was being dragged over to one of the *salon's workstations*. By now, he was kicking and squeaking. But Tidytail was all business.

"We have an emergency here!" he shrieked to his staff. "This customer needs a complete makeover! And I mean

MAKEOVER! We start with an **EXFOLIATING** Swiss scrub. Then a *moisturizing*

"WHAT A MESS!"

mozzarella cream. And finally, a shredded-cheddar mud **mask**."

TWO HOURS later, Trap was finished with Phase One of his makeover. I must say, his snout was glowing. Of course, by now he had finally figured out what was going on. He looked like he wanted to escape any way he could. But he didn't have a chance. Not with Tidytail around. That mouse was a regular furball of energy! He raced over to Trap and shoved him into a pink **padded** chair. Then he began combing through Trap's fur. "What a mess!" he declared. "So many split ends! So many fleas!"

Trap didn't say a word. His face was fixed in a permanent scowl.

"First of all, you'll need a super-strength flea RINSE," Tidytail advised. "Then a nourishing cream cheese conditioning treatment. And we'll have to put in some curls. Then, of course, we'll need to change this drab color. Miss Ratmousen is a blonde, correct?"

Trap just grumbled. **Grrrr...**

A Dusting of
Powder on the Tail

Tidytail squeaked on and on. Two hours later, he was finished with the fur. Next, it was time for makeup. Tidytail pulled out a pair of long tweezers. "First, we must pluck these eyebrows," he insisted, leaning over Trap. He looked like a mad rat surgeon operating on a patient.

My cousin was out of his chair in a flash. "**DON'T TOUCH ME!**" he squeaked. But Tidytail was already finished.

He pulled out a blush brush and stroked Trap's cheeks. While he worked, he kept checking out a picture taped to his wall. It was a photo of Sally Ratmousen.

"Let's see, we'll need false eyelashes," he

mumbled. "Then the **LIPSTICK** and nail polish. And, of course, a dusting of the finest powder on the tail."

After that, he gave Trap a pair of contact lenses. They were the exact color of Sally's eyes—ice-blue! Then

RATEL
N°5
SAN MOUSCISCO
EAU DE PARFUM

he sprayed Trap with some perfume. Finally, he called the fancy dress shop where Sally bought all of her clothes. He ordered an outfit for my cousin. When it arrived, Tidytail whisked Trap away to a back room.

Minutes later, Timothy called us in. "Come and see! He is a work of art!" he squeaked proudly.

I couldn't believe my eyes. My cousin *was* a work of art. A work of art named Sally Ratmousen!

My cousin Trap before his makeover . . .

. . . and after!

ATTENTION:
THIS MAY LOOK LIKE
SALLY RATMOUSEN, BUT
IT'S REALLY TRAP!

YOUR BILL, SIR!

Trap stood up. He studied himself in the mirror. "Do I really look like her?" he asked.

Tidytail clapped his paws. "You look exactly like her. Maybe even *better*! Much more glamorous, more attractive, more charming!"

Trap shot him a puzzled look.

Tidytail didn't seem to notice. He was too busy printing out the bill. When he was done, he slapped it into my paw.

I stared at the total. I felt faint. My paws began to shake. My tail began to twitch. I had to sit down in the pink chair to keep from falling. I had never seen such a bill. A furcut cost more than six months' worth of cheddar! A massage cost more than my entire set of the Encyclopaedia Ratannica!

I started to complain, but Thea cut me off. I guess she could tell I was in shock. "Don't you dare embarrass me!" she hissed. "**Fur 4 Life** is the most exclusive salon in the city. It's worth every penny. Just pay the bill, Geronimo. And don't forget the tip!"

I handed over **A WAD OF MONEY**. I couldn't believe I was doing it. I could have bought a new car with all of that money. Instead, I had bought my cousin a new look. And he wasn't even happy about it. He stepped on my tail on his way out the door. Tears rolled down my fur. I didn't know if I was crying because of the pain or because my wallet was empty.

Outside, a well-dressed female mouse

waved to Trap. "Sally, dear!" she called. "We must do lunch again soon! How does next week sound?"

My cousin opened his mouth to reply. Luckily, Thea stopped him in time. "Um, Ms. Ratmousen has lost her voice," she mumbled. "Yes, she has a terrible sore throat. She'll have to get back to you."

The mouse stared at Sally, I mean, Trap, closely. Did she notice anything different? Quickly, we shoved Trap into a taxi and drove home.

That night on television, Sally's snout appeared on the news. She was being interviewed by the famous reporter Bill Blabberat, Jr. "Tell me, Ms. Ratmousen," he began. "How does it feel to be the most important publisher on Mouse Island?"

Sally had a smug look on her face. She ripped the microphone out of Bill's paws.

"**It feels great!**" she squeaked. "*I am great!*"

Blabberat didn't know what to make of her. "Yes, well, why do you think Mr. Stilton sold you his paper at such a low price?" he continued.

Sally jumped up. "Because Geronimo Stilton is a cheesehead!" she shrieked. "And I am not. I am **SMART!** I am **SHARP!** I am the **MOST CLEVER** mouse in New Mouse City!"

"I am great!"

Bill Blabberat, Jr., coughed. He stared down at his notes.

Sally Ratmousen may have been clever, but she was also crazy! When Blabberat said *The Daily Rat* wasn't as polished as *The Rodent's Gazette,* Sally blew her top. She grabbed the Mouse TV reporter by the shirt. Then she shook him until his eyes rattled.

"**HELP!**" he shrieked.

I couldn't watch anymore. I switched off the set. I just had to get my paper back before that rotten Ratmousen ruined it!

Bill Blabberat, Jr.

I Am On My Way!

Trap spent the night watching videos of Sally. He practiced her walk. He practiced her voice. He even practiced her nasty sneer.

The next morning, we left for *The Daily Rat*. I was more nervous than a mouselet on his first day at squeaking school. Would our plan to win back *The Rodent's Gazette* work?

Thea parked her car by the entrance. Then Benjamin called Sally on Thea's cell phone. He told her he was a big fan. "In fact, I have started a **FAN CLUB** in your honor," my nephew squeaked. "We are throwing a party for you right now. Listen to the crowd!"

Benjamin held out the phone. The rest of us screamed and cheered.

"Ratmousen rules!

Stilton stinks!"

we shrieked.

My nephew grinned. "I hope you'll join us, Ms. Ratmousen," he said. "We're at 35 Cheddar Court."

There was silence on the line. I held my breath. Would Sally buy our story? It was pretty unbelievable. Who would throw a party for a rotten mouse like Sally?

"Well, I wouldn't want to disappoint my fans!" Sally finally answered. "I'm on my way!"

Who would buy our unbelievable story? A rotten mouse named Sally Ratmousen!

TELL IT TO SOME MOUSE WHO CARES!

A few minutes later, Sally rushed out of the building. She headed for a taxi. Just then, a shy-looking mouse stopped her. "Sorry to bother you, Ms. Ratmousen," the mouse squeaked. "I'm Mickey Misprint, your proofreader. I just wanted to ask you about my raise. You've been telling me I would get one for the past ten years. I have five small mice to feed, and we live in a tiny hole. Some nights we go to bed hungry."

Sally pushed him away. "Puh-lease!" she snorted. "I don't have time for your little problem." Then she began to imitate Mickey in a high-pitched voice. "I'm a *FAMOUSE* mouse, a **RICH** and **IMPORTANT** rodent. I don't have time for your petty concerns," she scoffed. "Tell it to some mouse who cares! I have a party to attend! **Now** get lost! **Right now! At once! Immediately!**"

Mickey Misprint's five children!

Poor Mickey wiped a tear from his eye. Then he slumped back into the building.

I was furious. Sally was so insensitive. At *The Rodent's Gazette,* I treat my employees with respect. We are all part of a team. I couldn't run the paper without them. Who did Sally think she was? I wanted to grab her by the tail and shake her.

Vrummmmmmmmmmmmmmmmm!

But she had already disappeared in a taxi.

Seconds later, Trap put Phase 2 of our plan into action. "Break a paw!" the rest of us whispered as he headed into the building. Then we snuck in behind him.

Near the staircase, Trap ran into Sally's managing editor, Rodney Rulerat. He had a stack of papers in his paws.

"Good morning, Ms. Ratmousen! Here are the stories you asked for. Do you want to read them now or later?" he mumbled.

Trap took a deep breath. Then, in perfect Sally form, he began to shout: "Now, you pinhead! Right now! At once! Immediately!

Well, what are you waiting for? I'm getting gray fur! Fork them over, Cheesebrain!"

Rodney didn't seem the least surprised. I guess he was used to Sally screaming at him.

He gave her the stories and scampered off.

Trap turned toward us and winked. The three of us gave a sigh of relief. So far, our plan was working like a charm!

Trap stormed down the hall. We followed right behind.

The offices of *The Daily Rat* were cold and bare. There didn't seem to be any coffee or soda machines. And all of the employees crept around, quiet as mice. They looked like they were afraid of their own furry shadows. When Sally, I mean, the fake Sally, strode by, you could practically feel the whole room tremble.

Pasted on the walls were framed sayings. Who wrote them? You guessed it — Sally Ratmousen!

Don't make me squeak!

Sally Ratmousen

WORK HARDER, WORK FASTER! JUST WORK!

Sally Ratmousen

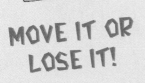

I CALL THE SHOTS AROUND HERE!

Trap found a door with a golden name plate on the front. It read,

Sally Ratmousen:
The Greatest Mouse on Earth

"I think she took too many confidence-building classes," Thea whispered.

I snickered. Sally really was incredible. Incredibly conceited, that is!

Trap marched through the door. The rest of us trailed behind.

Sally's office was a huge, icy room. **Brr!** It was bigger than my entire mouse hole. Her desk was an enormous triangular glass table. The legs looked just like three cat's paws.

Sally's desk was an enormous triangular glass table.

Trap plopped down in Sally's armchair. Then he buzzed the secretary. *"Bring me Geronimo Stilton's contract, please,"* he said.

Uh-oh, I groaned to myself. What was he doing? Why had he been so polite? Sally would never say "please." She was too rude.

There was silence on the other end. Then the secretary spoke. "Ms. Ratmousen?" she squeaked, sounding puzzled. "Is that you?"

Trap immediately realized he had made a mistake. "Of course it's me, you fool!" he screeched in his best Sally voice. "What is wrong with you? Are your ears lined with cheese? **Get me that contract right now! At once!** *Immediately!*"

I grinned. Now, that was much better. Trap was really getting into his role. He sounded exactly like the Sally I knew and feared! Hmm. Maybe Trap should think about a new career as an actor.

Thirty seconds later, a folder lay on the glass table. In it was the sale contract of *The Rodent's Gazette*!

Right now!
At once!
Immediately!

GET LOST, CHEDDARFACE!

Next, my cousin called downstairs to the security guardrat. "Clear the fur out of your ears and listen carefully," he ordered. "A mouse who looks exactly like me is on her way here. Tell her I am the real Ratmousen. The main mouse. The genuine article. And I don't want to be disturbed!"

Just then, we heard shouting outside. Trap opened the window and peeked out.

"It's **Sally**," he whispered to us. "She's using the guardrat as her own personal trampoline! Now she's biting his tail. Now she's pulling out his whiskers. Cheese niblets! She's one angry mouse!"

Seconds later, my cousin leaned out the

window. He smiled and waved to Sally. "Get lost, Cheddarface!" he shrieked with glee. "Now I call the shots around here!"

"She's using the guardrat as her own personal trampoline!"

THIS IS ALL YOUR FAULT!!

We got to work immediately. First, we wrote up a new contract. In this one, Sally gave *The Rodent's Gazette* back to me.

Then Trap called every  TV station in New Mouse City. Reporters came by the dozens. Dressed as Sally, my cousin made these announcements:

1. *The Rodent's Gazette* will be returned to Geronimo Stilton.

2. *The Daily Rat* will sponsor a contest for new writers. All stories will be read by Geronimo Stilton. Each month, he will award a prize to the best new talent. The prize will be paid for by *The Daily Rat*.

3. *The Daily Rat* will triple the salary of all of its employees. It will also send its employees on a first-class vacation to the Mousehamas.

I grinned. The Mousehamas was my idea. Sally didn't believe in vacations. Her workers needed some fun in the sun!

When the reporters left, Trap called the secretary. "Call the most expensive cheese shop in town," he ordered. "I'm throwing a party for all of the rodents who work here. **Right now! At once! *Immediately!***"

The secretary gasped. "Are y-y-you f-f-f-feeling OK, Ms. Ratmousen?" she stammered.

Trap pounded the desk with his paw. "Of

Long live Sally

course I'm feeling OK, you fool!" he squeaked. "Call that cheese shop **right now! At once! Immediately!**"

Five minutes later, the food arrived. A huge table was set up in the courtyard outside. Soon, the party was going strong.

Suddenly, I heard a noise. It was a bird. It was plane. No, it was an army tank! That's right, an army tank driven by the real **Sally Ratmousen!** She

was so mad that steam was rising from her fur.

We hid under a table. Sally climbed out of the tank. Reporters crowded around her. They began firing questions. Sally barely had time to squeak.

"Ms. Ratmousen, why have you given *The Rodent's Gazette* back to Stilton?" asked one reporter.

Sally went pale.

"Ms. Ratmousen, why are you throwing this expensive party?" asked another.

Sally's left eye began to twitch.

Meanwhile, the employees of *The Daily Rat* were busy dancing their paws off. They waved and cheered at Sally.

"Thank you for the raise! Thank you for the vacation! Thank you for the party, Boss!" they cried.

Sally stamped her paw. She looked as if she

were ready to burst. "Raise? Vacation? Party?" she thundered. "Have you all gone **crazy?**"

Just then, a very familiar-looking pair of ears and whiskers peeped out of the tank. It was me — I mean, it was my lookalike, **Sydney StarFur!**

Sally pushed him back in with her paw. "This is all your fault, **StarFur!**" she shrieked. "I knew you didn't look enough like Geronimo Stilton!"

"This is all your fault, Star" "This is all your fault, Starfur!" "This is all your fault, Starfur!" "This is all your fault, Starfur!" "This is all your fault, Starfur!" "This is all your fault, Star

STORIES BY
THE TON!

Do you want to know how it all ended?
Of course you do, or you wouldn't be
reading this!

Well, Sally went back to running **THE
DAILY RAT**. But she had to keep all of the
promises she had made. She paid her
employees lots more money. And they all
had a fabumouse time in the Mousehamas.

What happened with the *writing
contest*? It was a huge success. I am
constantly receiving new stories. There are

so many talented writers out there. I could write a whole book about them!

One day, a rodent named **FRANZ RATKA** came to see me. He was very thin and had huge ears. He said he hadn't left his mouse hole in years. I gasped. His cheese delivery bill must have been enormous! Ratka said he had written a book, *THE METAMORPHOSIS*, about a mouse who wakes up one morning and discovers he has turned into a bug! It was fascinating.

Another day, I met a mouse named **EDGAR ALLAN PAW**. He had a mustache and deep-set eyes. He brought me a spooky poem called "**The Raven**." And another story about a mouse and a beating heart. It was horribly scary. Still, I couldn't put it down.

Then I met a little old lady mouse named

Agatha Ratsie. She was small and spoke with a soft squeak. I was surprised to find out she wrote murder mysteries. Such a sweet, frail mouse. I guess you can't always tell a mouse by her squeak. Agatha wrote some wonderful thrillers. My favorite was called MOUSER ON THE ORIENT EXPRESS.

I was in the middle of a story by a writer named **CHEWS DICKENS** when my sister popped into my office. She dumped another

EDGAR ALLAN PAW

FRANZ RATKA

huge pile of stories on my desk. How would I ever have time to read them? Oh, I'm not complaining. I mean, I love publishing books. And, of course, my newspaper, *The Rodent's Gazette*, is my pride and joy. Still, being a publisher is hard work. Really hard work.

"Don't forget that at six o'clock you have that CHEESE AND THE MEANING OF LIFE lecture," Thea reminded me now. "And then at seven-thirty you have that FAMOUS FURBALLS OF

Agatha Ratsie

CHEWS DICKENS

OUR TIME conference. And then at nine you are giving that SELF-DEFENSE FOR THE MEEK AND MILD MOUSE speech at New Mouse University."

I sighed.

Thea kept on squeaking. She told me she had received a call from Sydney StarFur. It seemed Sally had lied to him. She had told Sydney that she was my childhood friend. He had thought he was hired to play an innocent joke on me. He had no idea about the evil plan Sally had cooked up. He had called to apologize.

"He sounds like a very nice mouse," Thea explained. "Look, he even gave us two free tickets to his show! It starts in twenty minutes. You'd better get moving!"

Right then, there was a knock at the door. Mickey Misprint, Sally's proofreader, came in.

He was working for me now. Of course, I was paying him a much higher salary. Mickey's family would never go hungry again.

"Mr. Stilton," he squeaked now, panting. "Here are more stories for you. In fact, here are tons more."

He piled them everywhere. On my desk. On my couch. On my furry cat rug.

More stories? How could I possibly read all of them?

I didn't even have time to comb my fur anymore!

Just then, my secretary, Mousella, buzzed me. "Your taxi is here, Mr. Stilton!" she announced. I looked up with a start.

Suddenly, the phone rang. "Mr. Stilton, we are expecting you tomorrow evening at the *Press Club*," the caller squeaked. "Don't let us down!"

I sighed. I had become such a celebrity that everyone wanted to interview me. I went to **parties**, lectures, business presentations. It was nice to feel wanted. Still, it was getting to be a problem. I mean, I am only one mouse. I cannot be in two places at once.

Right then, I caught sight of my

reflection in the windowpane.

Hmm. Maybe I could be in two places at once. All I had to do was find another Geronimo Stilton. He would have to look just like me. He would have to walk just like me. He would have to squeak just like me. . . .

Cheesecake! It seemed like a very good idea, I decided.

But that's another story. . . .

ABOUT THE AUTHOR

Born in New Mouse City, Mouse Island, Geronimo Stilton is Rattus Emeritus of Mousomorphic Literature and of Neo-Ratonic Comparative Philosophy. For the past twenty years, he has been running *The Rodent's Gazette*, New Mouse City's most widely read daily newspaper.

Stilton was awarded the Ratitzer Prize for his scoop on *The Curse of the Cheese Pyramid*. He has also received the Andersen 2000 Prize for Personality of the Year. One of his bestsellers won the 2002 eBook Award for world's best ratlings' electronic book. His works have been published all over the globe.

In his spare time, Mr. Stilton collects antique cheese rinds and plays golf. But what he most enjoys is telling stories to his nephew Benjamin.

Don't miss any of my other fabumouse adventures!

#1 Lost Treasure of the Emerald Eye

#2 The Curse of the Cheese Pyramid

#3 Cat and Mouse in a Haunted House

and coming soon

#4 I'm Too Fond of My Fur!

#5 Four Mice Deep in the Jungle

#7 Red Pizzas for a Blue Count

Want to read my next adventure?
It's sure to be a fur-raising experience!

RED PIZZAS FOR A BLUE COUNT

My troublemaker cousin was trapped in Transratania! And before I could even squeak, my sister, Thea, dragged me along on her rescue mission. Little did we know that Transratania is the land of vampire bats! Holey cheese, bats give me mouse bumps! Why? Well, there's nothing a bat likes more than sinking its teeth into a nice, juicy mouse. . . .

THE RODENT'S GAZETTE

1. **Main Entrance**
2. **Printing presses** (where the books and newspaper are printed)
3. **Accounts department**
4. **Editorial room** (where the editors, illustrators, and designers work)
5. **Geronimo Stilton's office**
6. **Storage space for Geronimo's books**

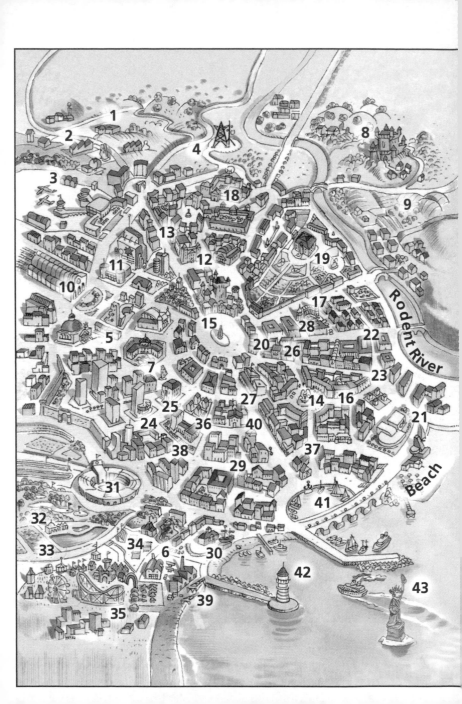

Map of New Mouse City

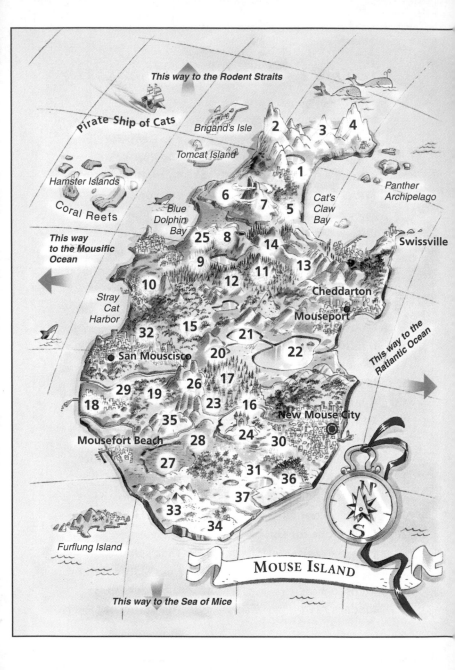

Map of Mouse Island

1. Big Ice Lake
2. Frozen Fur Peak
3. Slipperyslopes Glacier
4. Coldcreeps Peak
5. Ratzikistan
6. Transratania
7. Mount Vamp
8. Roastedrat Volcano
9. Brimstone Lake
10. Poopedcat Pass
11. Stinko Peak
12. Dark Forest
13. Vain Vampires Valley
14. Goose Bumps Gorge
15. The Shadow Line Pass
16. Penny Pincher Lodge
17. Nature Reserve Park
18. Las Ratayas Marinas
19. Fossil Forest
20. Lake Lake
21. Lake Lake Lake
22. Lake Lakelakelake
23. Cheddar Crag
24. Cannycat Castle
25. Valley of the Giant Sequoia
26. Cheddar Springs
27. Sulfurous Swamp
28. Old Reliable Geyser
29. Vole Vail
30. Ravingrat Ravine
31. Gnat Marshes
32. Munster Highlands
33. Mousehara Desert
34. Oasis of the Sweaty Camel
35. Cabbagehead Hill
36. Tropical Jungle
37. Rio Mosquito

Dear mouse friends,
thanks for reading, and farewell
till the next book.
It'll be another whisker-licking-good
adventure, and that's a promise!

Geronimo Stilton